P9-CFA-629

Little Bear's Surprise

written by Kathleen Allan Meyer

illustrated by Carol Boerke

Library of Congress Catalog Card No. 88-63573
Published by The STANDARD PUBLISHING Company, Cincinnati, Ohio
Division of STANDEX INTERNATIONAL Corporation. Printed in U.S.A.

Autumn had already come to the forest. The cold wind sent little red and yellow leaf airplanes whirling to the ground. They made deep, deep piles.

Little Bear and his brothers tumbled through them. Then they jumped into the biggest pile!

"Winter will soon be here," Mother Bear called to the cubs. "It is just about time for all good bears to go to sleep."

"We don't want to go to sleep," Little Bear said.

Beartram agreed. "We're having too much fun!"

"If you will go to sleep now," Mother Bear replied, "I will wake you up for a Valentine's Day party on February 14. Usually we sleep a little longer than that."

"What's Valentine's Day?" Little Bear asked.

"Valentine's Day is celebrated to let others know how much we love them," Mother Bear answered.

"Sometimes special cards or presents are given to others. And it's always fun to have a party.

"Now run on home and we'll make some valentines before we go to sleep."

So off they went, hurrying home.

Beartram and Alfred had no problem making their cards.

Snip, snip, snip went their scissors as they cut out lovely red heart shapes.

Then they squeezed the glue bottles hard. Out came the sticky white stuff to glue the hearts together.

Soon Beartram and Alfred had a pile of the loveliest, laciest valentines in the whole, wide world.

But Little Bear was not able to make any valentines, even though Mother Bear helped him. She showed him how to hold the scissors. But his little paws were just not big enough yet. Neither were they strong enough to squeeze out the glue.

Little Bear felt very sad. There were so many things he wasn't able to do!

That evening Mother Bear pushed open the bark door of their home. She looked out to see what the weather was like.

"It's snowing! It's snowing!" she exclaimed. "How cozy it makes our home!"

And Little Bear and his brothers ran to the door. They saw the big, feathery flakes of snow falling gently to the ground. This was the first time they had ever seen snow.

"Now I *know* it's bedtime," said Mother Bear.

Beartram and Alfred were excited. They didn't mind going to bed. The next time they woke up, it would be Valentine's Day. Then they would have a party and give out their beautiful cards!

But Little Bear was very sad. When *he* woke up, he would have nothing to give!

"Pleasant dreams," said Mother Bear as she kissed all of them good-night.

"I hope you dream something special, Little Bear," she added.

Soon Little Bear drifted off to sleep. And he did dream something *very* special. He dreamed about what he could give his mother and brothers at the party.

To make sure they would wake up on Valentine's Day, Mother Bear placed her calendar beside the bed. And each morning as she turned over and opened one eye, she put her pawprint on the day's date.

Before she knew it, February 14 had come!

"Wake up, wake up, everyone," she said, "party day is here!"

The cubs jumped out of bed. They were ready for the party.

"Now cover your eyes, please," said Mother Bear. "I have a surprise for you."

From a dark corner of their cozy cave she brought out a big honeycomb. It was dripping with delicious golden honey! She set it on their tree stump table.

Little Bear's eyes danced with delight. It had been a long time since he'd had honey.

"Now let's give out our valentines," Mother Bear said.

So they all ran to get their lovely, lacey valentines, except Little Bear. He didn't have any. So he just stood there and waited.

"I have a riddle," said Beartram.
"What is red and lacey
And opens up
And you give it on Valentine's Day
To say, 'I love you?'"
"Is it a beautiful valentine?" guessed Mother Bear.
"Yes," shouted Beartram. Then he gave everyone a card.

"I have a riddle, too," said Alfred.
"What is pink and lavender and white
And stands up by itself
And you only give it on Valentine's Day?"
"A lovely valentine," the others guessed.
"Right on!" said Alfred.

Then they all looked at Little Bear. He had no valentines behind *his* back.

"Don't worry about me," he said, "because I have a riddle, too!"

"What is it?" they all asked in surprise.

"What's warm and soft
And you don't wrap it up
You wrap it around
And it's good for any time of the year
Not just on Valentine's Day?"

"We don't know the answer. We give up," they all said.

Quickly Little Bear ran first to his mother, and next to each of his brothers, and gave them a Little Bear Hug!

Then they all sat down for the sweetest feast of honey they'd ever had!